BAGDASARIAN
P R O D U C T I O N S

ALVINNN!!!
AND THE CHIPMUNKS™
Alvin and the Superheroes

adapted by Lauren Forte
based on the screenplay "Superheroes"
written by Reid Harrison

Ready-to-Read

Simon Spotlight

New York   London   Toronto   Sydney   New Delhi

SIMON SPOTLIGHT
An imprint of Simon & Schuster Children's Publishing Division
1230 Avenue of the Americas, New York, New York 10020
This Simon Spotlight edition August 2017
Alvin and The Chipmunks, The Chipettes and Characters TM & © 2017 Bagdasarian
Productions, LLC. All rights reserved. Licensed by PGS HK Ltd. All Rights Reserved.
All rights reserved, including the right of reproduction in whole or in part in any form.
SIMON SPOTLIGHT, READY-TO-READ, and colophon are registered trademarks of
Simon & Schuster, Inc.
For information about special discounts for bulk purchases, please contact
Simon & Schuster Special Sales at 1-866-506-1949 or business@simonandschuster.com.
Manufactured in the United States of America 0717 LAK
10 9 8 7 6 5 4 3 2 1
ISBN 978-1-5344-0010-8 (hc)
ISBN 978-1-5344-0009-2 (pbk)
ISBN 978-1-5344-0011-5 (eBook)

"I'm a superhero!" Theodore shouted as he ran around in his homemade costume.
"My name is the Cackler! Ha-ha-ha-ha!"

"*Boo!*" Alvin yelled,
trying to scare him.
Theodore screamed loudly.
Alvin shook his head.
"Rule number one: Superheroes don't
scream like babies. And rule number
two: Superheroes never give up."

Theodore was amazed.
"How do you know so much
about superheroes?" he asked.
"Simple," Alvin whispered.
"I am a superhero."

Alvin dashed into his closet
and came back out wearing
a superhero mask.
"Behold the Dark Shadow!"

"I want you to teach me everything!" cried Theodore. Alvin thought for a minute. "Superhero training starts with . . . cleaning my room. Cleaning will help you become quick."

Theodore spent the
next hour racing around.
He picked up clothes.

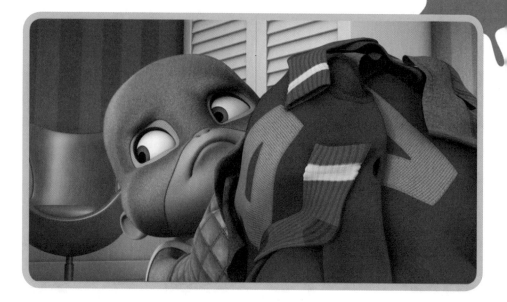

He washed the dishes.

He did all the yard work.

He even washed Dave's car!

"Alvin, are you making Theodore
do your chores *again*?"
Simon asked when he walked by.
"The chores are teaching him how
to be a superhero," Alvin insisted.

Simon was not convinced.
As Alvin and Theodore
moved on to the next chore,
Simon asked, "What happens
when Theodore wants to
fight real villains?"

"Fight villains? Yay! When?"
exclaimed Theodore.
"Um, why not tonight?" said Alvin.
Theodore ran off to get ready.

Simon frowned at Alvin. "You know you're not really superheroes, right?" "You're right," said Alvin. "We need a villain. That's where you come in." "Oh no," Simon replied.

Later that night Alvin
and Theodore put on their
superhero costumes. Then
they went to look for bad guys.
Simon hid in an alleyway,
dressed up as a supervillain
called the Pieman.

"Give me that necklace
or else!" Simon shouted,
pretending to rob someone.
Alvin and Theodore ran
toward him, ready to fight.

Suddenly, a pie came flying
out of the darkness.
It hit a wall next to them.

"Go get him, Cackler!"
Alvin yelled.
Theodore took a deep breath
and ran into the shadows.

While Theodore tried to find
the thief, Simon ran out of
the alley. He handed Alvin a pie
and went home.
"He's gone, Cackler! Great work!"
Alvin called into the alley as he
smashed the pie on his own face.

"Dark Shadow!" Theodore said
when he saw Alvin.
"A-Are you okay?!"
"Yeah," Alvin muttered.
"But . . . he pied me."
"No!" Theodore cried.

When they got home, Theodore
asked, "When are we going
to fight more villains?"
Alvin and Simon were tired.
They could not make up
fake crime fights like this
every night!

Simon spoke up first.

"Enough. Theodore, I was Pieman."

"You're a criminal?" asked Theodore.

"I'm *not* a criminal," Simon said.

"Alvin and I made up
the whole thing."

"So . . . I'm not a superhero?"
Theodore asked sadly.
"None of us are," Alvin admitted.
"But we had fun, right?"
Theodore was so disappointed.

Later that night Theodore
snuck out of bed.
"Rule number two," he said
as he put on his Cackler costume,
"a superhero never gives up.
Ha-ha-ha."

When Theodore left the house,
he saw a suspicious man.
"Robbing the museum?"
Theodore muttered quietly.
"We'll just see about that!
Ha-ha-ha."

In the museum Theodore hit the alarm that called the police.

Then he ran to find the robber. But soon he realized the man wasn't a robber at all. It was just the museum's janitor!

The janitor was startled when
he saw Theodore.
He threw Theodore into a closet.
But when Theodore turned on his
flashlight, he saw a *real*
robber in the closet with him.
Back at home Alvin and Simon
woke up and found a note
on Theodore's bed.

The note said that Theodore
had left to fight crime!
They ran to get Dave.

Dave, Alvin, and Simon
searched until they noticed
police cars at the museum.
Inside, a police officer
was asking the janitor
about the alarm. He thought
the janitor was the robber!

"Don't worry, everyone.
I caught the robber!"
called Theodore from
the hallway.
"There was no robber," Simon called.
"It was just the janitor."

"Not *that* robber!" yelled Theodore.
"The one in here!" Theodore stepped
aside, revealing the real robber,
now all tied up.
"He was trying to escape
when I surprised him,"
Theodore explained.

The police officer shook Theodore's
hand. "Good work! But next time
you see something suspicious,
report it to the police first."
The Cackler smiled. "Yes, sir!"

A few days later everyone knew about the Cackler's heroic adventure. Alvin wanted in on the fame.

"Hey, Theodore, you and I should go solve more crimes!"

Theodore thought for a moment.

"Well, okay, but you're going to need some training first!"